The Bird Who Made Good

BOOKS BY ELSWYTH THANE

FICTION

RIDERS OF THE WIND
ECHO ANSWERS
CLOTH OF GOLD
HIS ELIZABETH
BOUND TO HAPPEN
QUEEN'S FOLLY
TRYST
REMEMBER TODAY
FROM THIS DAY FORWARD
DAWN'S EARLY LIGHT
YANKEE STRANGER
LIGHT HEART

NON-FICTION

THE TUDOR WENCH
YOUNG MR. DISRAELI
ENGLAND WAS AN ISLAND ONCE
THE BIRD WHO MADE GOOD

PLAYS

THE TUDOR WENCH
YOUNG MR. DISRAELI

CHEEWEE

The Bird
Who Made Good

BY ELSWYTH THANE

Drawings by Don R. Eckleberry

DUELL, SLOAN and PEARCE
New York

First edition

Printed in the United States of America

To

*His Father and his Mother, and his
Sisters and his Cousins and his Aunts,
who each year return to feast on our
seeds and nest in our evergreens*

The Bird Who Made Good

1.

AT FIRST HE DIDN'T
even have a name. He was as unwelcome as that.

For weeks after I had impatiently shoved on a rain-
coat and tied something over my head and run out into
a driving storm to pick up the little ball of wet down
and feathers which was making feeble, foot-high flops

9

across our Vermont lawn, he was known simply as "the bird" and sometimes with a grudging admiration for his infant aplomb as "feller." He was going to be a nuisance and we didn't want to bother with him. We would only get fond of him and then he would die. We hadn't a cage to put him in and we didn't approve of caged birds anyway, and he was sure to mess up the books and the upholstery. He couldn't possibly be taken back to New York with us in the autumn, as the apartment was full of valuable books and Chinese embroideries. We didn't want a pet, we moved around too much, somebody was always away. So when the weather cleared, if he lived that long, he would just have to look after himself outdoors.

But meanwhile we were stuck with him, and we resented the endless amount of time it seemed to take to feed him his diet of bread soaked in milk, hard-boiled egg yolk, and orange juice. The bread had to be pushed down his throat with forceps and the orange juice was poured in from a medicine dropper, as he had no idea of feeding himself and simply sat there with his beak open and yelled. If he wasn't fed often enough he yelled till somebody came. If he woke up in the morning before we did he yelled till somebody came. His voice was high and sweet and tireless—and carried well. We got awfully sick of him, and he went right on living and loving it.

He was too interested to die. He wasn't afraid of us, he liked his food and his cracker-box lined with Kleenex to sleep in, and he liked being in a warm house where the rain couldn't wet him. He was to the manor born, and nothing, but *nothing,* could upset his dignity.

Resignedly, since we might as well do it right, we read up on his kind. We deduced by the pattern of his brown feathers and his stout beak and scruffy crest, and by the presence of a male purple finch in the cherry hedge behind the house, that that was his kind. And we learned from the book what he was supposed to eat, and brought him bouquets of sorrel and chickweed and blue-grass seeds, and he learned to pick at them for himself, and to drink from a glass ashtray. When presented with another ashtray full of canary seed he soon grasped what to do about that too. We had to admit that he was pretty smart for his age. He graduated from the cracker-box to sleep less mussily on a branch fastened inside a cylinder of chicken-wire which could be covered with a dark cloth to keep him quiet in the mornings till the family was up, and which would also protect him from possible mice.

His feathers grew, his frowsy bits of baby down gradually disappeared, last of all two horns of fluff on his head which rose with his crest and looked pretty ridiculous, and the wide yellow gapers at the sides of his bill became less noticeable. But the weather went on being the same kind of blustery, wet, cold weather that had dumped him on the lawn in the beginning, with pitiless winds. Every time it cleared up for a few hours we discussed turning him out to the normal hazards of a

Vermont bird's life, and every time threatening banks of cloud over the mountain reprieved him, and every time during the ensuing storm somebody would say, "Well, it's a good thing we didn't put him out into this."

And the bird, perching on a lilac branch fastened to the upper sill of a window, would survey the drenched, chilly world beyond the protecting glass with complacent interest. And then, just to make sure, he would go and sit on the lower rung of a chair, or under the overhang of a lamp-shade, and there preen and oil his feathers with great care, in case he got wet after all. Yes, he was funny—but we didn't intend to fall for it.

He enjoyed everything that went on, especially gatherings around the fire at tea time, and he listened attentively to all the conversation, facing the company from a nearby chair-back or lamp-shade, definitely one of the party, entering wholly into the spirit of the thing. He loved people, and furniture, and trying to snitch food no bird should have; he loved music on the radio, and sat close to it, expressing appreciation and contentment by hoisting up one foot into his breast feathers and bunching himself cosily; he loved riding on people's shoulders—always facing frontwards; he loved to sit in the window and watch down the road for visitors, even though it was a private road and not much happened on it except the ice-man and the baker and the milk-and-eggs. Once the man who brought the bottled gas sailed by in his big blue truck without slacking speed till he got to the turn-around in the barnyard, which was all quite noisy and surprising, and caused the window-sill kibitzer to go straight up in the air with a startled *yeep* and land on my shoulder a few feet away, where apparently he felt safe. But it wasn't long until every time he heard a car coming up the road he would fly to the window to see it go by, with no sign of fear. Just twice when he was very small he flew against the glass, and then he had learned forever, and never tried to go through it again.

He even loved the typewriter. I was trying to finish the final draft of a manuscript by at least an approximate date, as I nearly always am, and a certain amount of concentration and undistracted working time was desirable. But the bird accompanied me to my attic study and sat on another lilac branch in the window there— these branch fixtures were designed to keep him off the furniture, and lilacs were best because it is fun for a bird to pinch off the leaves and see them fall, and when this has been done the bare branch is composed of many delightful little angled twigs and perching places.

For about an hour the first time he heard it the intermittent clatter of the typewriter worried him and he would elongate himself and peer round from his window vantage point. Then he decided it wasn't coming after him. And then he wanted to investigate. He flew down on to a picture-frame which stood near by on the big table where I work, and remarked "Che-*wee*?" which was about all the conversation he had. The typewriter went right on making a noise. During its next pause he flew down on to the ribbon-box, experimentally. I struck a key and he dashed back to the picture-frame with a resentful "Teet-a-teet-teet!" He waited till the carriage was still again and lit on the projecting lever which turns up the roller. I struck a key. He stayed. I hit two or three more and he couldn't take it. But he can now. Now he lands on the lever even when the carriage is in motion and clings there, his toes wrapped tight, his expression grim and determined, his wings a little loose to help him balance when the shift key jolts him, never flinching as the keys strike up past his beak. He seems to ride the typewriter carriage with the same kind of fearful joy that people get out of riding the roller coaster. It's inconvenient for me, of course, because I have to take hold of the wrong end of the roller to turn it up. But if there's anything in it for him, who am I to complain?

Oh, yes, he has won. All the way along, he has won. His name is Che-Wee, and he recognizes the sound of it, and will fly in from the next room—sometimes—if called.

2.

PERHAPS IT WAS HIS
self-possession that finally broke me down. He never
fluttered, even when my warm hand first closed over
him that wet day on the lawn. He never panicked and
fled at an unexpected movement, or dodged if something was passed above his head when he sat eating seeds

on a corner of the table. He would always step up obligingly on any forefinger which approached not-too-fast and nudged his tummy. He never regarded himself as a stranger here. It was his home, and we were his family, and our friends were his friends.

Or perhaps it was his curiosity. Anybody bent over doing something—particularly tieing or untieing a parcel—was irresistible to him, and he lit on a shoulder with an inquiring "Teet-a-teet-teet?" and from there often went to your hands and seized an end of the string or a corner of the paper helpfully. Fitting a picture into a frame, tieing shoelaces, snipping out a paragraph from a newspaper, sewing, even driving a nail—it was all some kind of game invented for his entertainment. Hammers didn't scare him. A hammer job sometimes meant that a fresh branch was being tacked up. He would rush to sit on it while it was still unsteady, while the hammer was still hitting the tacks. Something new! Mind you get it right, now. Jeepers, just what I wanted. Too many leaves, though, I'll see to that. . . . He would be busy for a long time, then, nipping off the base of the stem, munching up the joint, peering down to see where each severed leaf would land before tackling the next one.

He always knew what he wanted, and conveyed it firmly to the rather obtuse people he depended on to give it to him. Fastened to the upper window sill beneath his lilac branches there was a board wider than the sill, wide enough to hold a folded paper towel

sprinkled with gravel and seeds sprinkled on the gravel.
His soft food was given to him in small ashtray dishes,
and his bouquets were clipped to the branch with a
othespin. But if he took from your fingers something
as a raspberry which was too big for one bite, he
ould carry it to the dish and lay it down there, quite
ately, to finish. Skeptically we offered him seeds
sh beside the same kind of seeds sprinkled on the
. He always ate from the dish. Loose food was for
birds, maybe. He had had advantages. He knew
to behave. So we bought him some more ashtrays.
Where he would sleep, after he was no longer a
, was a problem he patiently solved for us himself.
makeshift chickenwire cage with a branch in it was
uisance and an eyesore, and he apparently hated it
much as we did. He had to be picked up each night
ter he had gone to roost somewhere round the room,
d set on the branch inside the wire. Each morning
hen the cloth was removed he hurried out and made
or his window sill branch with visible relief.

A sleeping place is very important to a bird, even
one who feels secure from the usual bird enemies. He
chose a clothes hook in a big closet off the downstairs
bathroom, and began to go there every night, tucking
himself up at twilight with his side leaned against the
comforting wooden strip into which the hook was
screwed, one foot cuddled into his feathers, head under
his wing. The closet was dark and warm and we closed
the door on him each evening and let him have it.

The Bird Who Made Good

But the house had a rebuilding program on, and the downstairs bathroom was being turned back into a bedroom with a lavatory in that closet, and a smaller upstairs bedroom was to become the bathroom. Che-Wee's little bedchamber had to have a window cut in it, and plumbing introduced. Ousted from his favorite refuge, he went to sleep in the oddest places—on a curtain-rod in the living-room with his head nearly touching the ceiling, on a row of books which left just room for him to squat on their tops with his head touching the shelf above—he wanted to be under something, and against something, he wanted a crotch or a roof.

There was a larger hook, the kind a plant-basket had once hung from, screwed into a closed door in a small alcove room where my correspondence desk was—a nook off the living-room furnished by me with a bookcase and a chest of drawers and a desk to provide what was described by an understanding guest as a place to brood in and pay one's bills. We fitted a square cardboard box, minus the front and one end, over that hook and against the door, at a height which would just touch his head if he sat up straight, and we extended the hook by tying on to it a branch to make a good landing-place. Che-Wee watched everything excitedly, lighting on our shoulders and hands, almost riding on the hammer. He knew at once that it was his, and that at last we had caught on. Almost before we had made it secure he took possession—sat on the branch about midway, combed out his feathers, tucked up one foot and had a doze—that night he slept there, leaned up against the back wall of the box, and every other night following. With the window-shade pulled down at dusk, and the other door closed, it was almost as good as the closet, and he was even better sheltered from owls or possible gales-in-the-night.

There was another thing he objected to about that bath-room job. It is an old house with the kind of open-air plumbing which leaves all the pipes exposed to view. Above the tub was a three-inch screw, with deeply scalloped edges, which was some kind of cut-off on the cold water pipe which ran up through the ceiling to the tank which stood then in the attic. In hot weather the pipe and screw were beaded with sweat, and Che-Wee had some idea that it was a good place to sit, even to spend the night. I thought it was a good place to catch pneumonia, and always shooed him off it, sometimes half a dozen times in an hour. I had to step into the bathtub and stretch to the limit of my reach to dislodge him, and it got to be quite a feud between us.

When the plumbing was removed from that room and it was papered and refurnished as a bedroom, the workmen neglected to fill up the two small holes in the ceiling where the pipes had gone through. Annoyed and efficient, I mixed some plaster and got a putty knife and spread newspapers on the bed beneath, which now replaced the bathtub, and climbed up to stuff the holes and plaster over them temporarily. I had no sooner begun than I was attacked by a furious small bird who

had apparently been nursing a grievance about that
vanished screw for days, and who associated my presence there now with the fact that it had been taken
away. He flew in at me from the next room and landed
on my shoulder in a whirlwind, uttering his "K-k-k-
k-k!" scolding note and pecking at my cheek and neck.
We had argued about that screw, it wasn't there any
more, and I was to blame, mucking about with plaster
where it had been.

3.

HE ASKED FOR A bath long before we thought he was old enough to know there was such a thing. As soon as he had learned to dip his beak into an ashtray full of water and dispense with the medicine dropper, he began to make bath-motions and throw drops of water over himself.

21

Astonished, I filled a small square dish with water and set it on a newspaper on the table. He hopped on the edge of the dish at once with an it's-about-time expression, and plopped down into the water and began to splash with his wings, his crest sticking straight up with delight.

His crest is like a dog's tail, it means everything, laughter much more than anger. Che-Wee laughs with the feathers on his head—when he wants to intimidate or challenge a hand that approaches his food he flattens himself like a little snake, makes threatening jabs with his beak and says "K-k-k-k-k!" He roared with laughter in that first bath, every feather on end, and spent a happy half hour preening himself afterwards. He has bathed joyfully almost every day since then, sometimes twice a day if the dish has not been put away. It's the most fun he has. And when he has soaked himself and everything within a radius of several feet, he rises noisily on wet pinions and comes to show me how clean he is, shaking a shower of spray over the desk.

Because we were so impressed at the early age at which he required a bathtub, we always encouraged and applauded him when he washed, egging him on with cries of "Attaboy!" and "Dunk yourself some more!" till it became a part of the bath-game and added to his excitement and self-importance. One day I was working at the desk and neglected to look up and comment when he began his bath. He dipped himself twice and then flew damply on to my shoulder with an insistent

The Bird Who Made Good

"Tswee?" I said, "That's no bath, go back and finish," and I took him on my finger and tossed him in the direction of his tub. He went back, jumped in, and splashed happily to the proper accompaniment of loud praise by me.

He taught us what he wanted to eat, too. If he had been a robin or a bluebird, we would have had less luck with his food and might not have raised him at all, not knowing which insects the parent birds would have brought to the nest and having less experience in catching them. But purple finches are first cousins to the canaries, and largely vegetarians, and thrive on the same kind of food that canaries want. When I was still feeding him with forceps I once tried a bit of cut-up earthworm. It went down all right, but the next time my hand came over him with another piece he wouldn't open his mouth. I discarded the earthworm and offered the familiar bread and milk. He opened up.

It was decorative to have a bird who ate flowers and grasses instead of beetles and worms. We simply brought him bouquets of things, from nasturtiums and forget-me-nots to timothy and caraway, and he chose what he wanted, resolutely ignoring some, going after others with great relish. Flower-fixing time was a great lark. I would bring in an armload of cosmos and golden-glow and phlox and lay it down on the table and bring vases full of water. In no time he was down on the heap of bloom, nipping out the stamens, biting the tubes of the phlox and nasturtiums where a drop of sweet could

23

be found. He would eat the center of a pansy and dissect a head of white clover, for the honey. He ate ripening seeds of caraway till he smelled of it. A tip of overgrown broccoli, half yellow flowers and half juicy buds, was wonderful fun. But after he came, no flowers which required treatment with insecticides, like zinnias, could come into the house for fear of making him sick. And no vase arrangement, however inspired, lasted long. He loved to sit on the long sprays of golden-glow, like the goldfinches outside, and demolish the flowers at the heart. It was very becoming to him, but it played the dickens with the mantelpiece decorations.

And we let him. He was winning.

He wasn't making the mess of the house we had expected him to, though. Seed-eaters are clean and odorless, and the spots he left were small and dry and usually brushed off the chintzes and rugs with very little damage. Books caught it badly a few times, and we made stiff cardboard squares to fit over the tops of the lamp-shades in the day time, and simple dusting wasn't enough. I hadn't set out to housebreak him, but gradually I realized that my natural reaction to brush him off and scold if he spotted my clothes or the papers on my desk was having an effect. More than once I saw him fly away from my shoulder or hands or table—just in time. Then I really went at it. Each time he made a mistake he was systematically, heartlessly brushed off and scolded. He notices the tone of voice, and his crest comes up and he bridles self-consciously and chews an end of the branch or wipes his beak—always with the effect of dusting off his hands—if extravagantly praised. Equally he knows if he is being scolded. At the age of eighteen months, he is pretty well shoulder-desk-and-manuscript-broken. Well, *hardly* ever. Sometimes he forgets and flies just afterwards instead of just before —aware that he is wrong, and uttering a hasty *yeep* as he goes.

He has made himself completely a member of the family and seems to know and even anticipate its daily routine. He is always on hand in the kitchen before breakfast to see the oranges cut and get his vitamins. He makes twittering, bustling flights from one end of the house to the other, turning corners with great dash and even learning to fly up and down a closed-in staircase. He supervises the dishwashing from a post on the towel-rack over the sink. When it is lunch time and preparations begin, he takes up a position on the back of a chair even before the table is laid, alert for snacks while the meal is put together. Peeling potatoes or tomatoes brings him down on your hands to snatch bits of peel off the edge of the knife, to the peril of his tongue and his toes. You can't cut an apple in two before he is there from clean across the room, *teet-a-teet-teet*, and crowding for the seeds. Knock a hard-boiled egg on the edge of the table or a bowl and he rushes in for a bite of the yolk, watching every move of your fingers hungrily while it is being peeled and cut. He will dance excitedly around an egg that hasn't been boiled if one is left lying on the table. Custards set out in individual dishes on a tray are likely to be scalloped with three-cornered bites before they reach the table. Radish tails are something to be carried away and gloated over, like raw peas, and he becomes secretive and greedy and round-shouldered over this kind of booty. He scolds furiously if a hand approaches while he is eating. A whole head of cabbage is not too big to nibble, and always, always the apple seeds, very special, which must be dug out of a cut core if it takes all day. Any fruit, raw or cooked, is irresistible—his Greek genus name, *Carpodacus*, means "fruit-biting."

In 1789 a German apothecary *cum* naturalist at Göttingen gave the name *Fringilla purpurea* to Che-Wee's ancestors, probably from a skin acquired for a natural history collection. This stuck until 1844 when DeKay called him *Erythrospiza purpurea*—the purple red sparrow. And finally the American Ornithological Union a half century later threw the book at him with *Carpodacus purpureus purpureus*, and there he is, twice purple and biting fruit. The English linnet is a near relative.

He seems to know when it is letter-writing time, and flies ahead of me when I start towards the alcove desk, arriving briskly on his favorite lamp-shade above it. From there he descends to the desk top to sample the erasers and pencil points and—if possible—the ink. I used to worry about his drinking ink, but if it was going to kill him he would be dead long ago. He chases the

pen-point as it travels across the paper, trying to catch
it in his beak, the way a kitten chases a stick, and allow-
ing it to drag him, feet braced and skidding, halfway
along a line. Or he lights accurately on the penholder
above my hand as I write and stays there, which re-
quires a nice adjustment of balance from both of us,
makes me a little less legible than normally, and sometimes rouses in me an uneasy suspicion that he can read.

He has always been a literary bird. If anyone sits
quietly reading a book he lights on the top of it and
chews little three-cornered bits out of the pages. When
you want to turn the leaf he will allow you to slip it
out from under his toes without dislodging him, or if
he is on the left-hand page he will step over the new
page when it touches his feet. An open newspaper chal-
lenges him to balance on the waversome upper edge until it collapses beneath him.

He has a sense of responsibility for us too. If somebody lies down on the sofa for a doze he comes and
sits on the back of it, or even on the sleeper's shoulder.
He sits very still, often with one foot tucked up in his
feathers in his own most relaxed and cosy state—but
without closing his eyes, as though he mounted guard.
If you rouse, he meets your gaze companionably. Eckstein in a delightful record of his canary family, men-
tions that they hated to be watched, and stopped what
they were doing if they felt his eyes on them, but I have
never noticed any shyness in Che-Wee. Even as a baby,
he looked into your face instead of at the hand which

fed him, if the hand was clumsy or slow. If you walk near him when he is on the floor he turns his head to look *up*, to see your face, instead of watching the foot which endangers him, and Eckstein noted the same thing in his birds. But an audience never disconcerts Che-Wee. In fact, he shows off.

4.

As THE FIRST SUM-
mer ended we realized that it would be impossible to
turn him out into the world. He was accustomed to
heated rooms and was too tender to endure a frosty
night. He hadn't flown enough to have the wing
strength for migration. And so we said that when we

went down to New York for the winter we would put him in the bird house at the Zoological Park, where he would have good care and company.

But by then I had begun to weaken, and I said I wished I hadn't got so fond of him, and it seemed rather like putting a child into an orphan asylum. The master of the house, who had been away when Che-Wee was brought in out of the storm and had met him only recently and was still holding out, said with noticeable resignation that he supposed he could bring down a cage from the Park and I could try it at the apartment and see if I felt like keeping Che-Wee there. I said with reservations that I thought I would like to try.

This was after Che-Wee had invented his card-trick. I never tried to teach him anything but manners; I hadn't time to fool around with him. But he was allowed to have meals out of his own dish on a mat on a corner of the table when we had ours. We were careful what he ate, and he was given a bit of raw salad or fruit, and a spoonful of milk in the bottom of a glass custard cup. He still drinks milk like a kitten; it was his baby food. One day to prevent him from stuffing himself before the rest of us were ready to sit down at the table, I laid a postcard over the top of the custard cup which contained the milk. I put it there while Che-Wee looked on disgustedly, thwarted and a-tiptoe. He surveyed the card with each eye separately, in an outraged and incredulous way. He made a tentative jab at it with his beak and the card moved. He then picked it up bodily and cast it aside, hopped on to the edge of the custard cup and helped himself to milk.

When I reported this feat to the master of the house, who has had forty years' experience with wild life both at home and in captivity, he gave me what is known as an old-fashioned look, and his lip curled slightly. I at once got a custard cup and some milk and a postcard. I let Che-Wee see me pour the milk and lay the card on top. Very high on his little stick legs, very straight in the chest, he hopped over, yanked off the card, and drank milk. "Well, I'll be darned!" said Dr. Beebe. I have heard a lot of unimpressionable people say somewhat the same thing since then, because Che-Wee doesn't forget his sole trick. He'll do it any time. When his original battered postcard, which had been sent from Hawaii by Grant Mitchell on a service tour with *Christopher Bean*, got mislaid and I resorted to a different one which hadn't got lovely blue water and Waikiki Beach on it, he dealt with it even more summarily, it seemed, because of its ugliness. Anything in the shape of a postcard or envelope lying flat on the table is likely to be twitched at impatiently in case there should be milk underneath.

His first migration southward was accomplished in a small cardboard box with air-holes punched in it, and he was in the train for five hours, arriving in New York after dark. Before taking him out of the box, I set out his familiar mat and seed dish, so that he would feel at home for his dinner. My husband watched me pityingly. "They never eat after travelling, and in a strange place," he said. And then Che-Wee bounced out of his box, hungry as a wolf, and went right to work on his seeds. He only wants a chance to demonstrate that the great naturalist doesn't know everything, and he'll come through like a ton of bricks.

My study where I work in New York can be closed off entirely from the rest of the apartment, and there we placed the large exhibition cage from the Zoo, on a table which was badly needed for a dozen other things, and introduced Che-Wee to it. He wasn't afraid of it, and he seemed to know that it belonged to him, and sat on top of it, and in the open door, and followed his seed dish inside it. But stay in it quietly with the door closed? Hunh-*unh*, think I'm one of those canaries?

Ten or fifteen minutes inside the cage is about his limit. Then he begins to pound from perch to perch and cling pathetically to the inside of the door. I tried to be firm. Once I left him shut in it and went shopping, hoping that he would resign himself eventually. When I returned he had so exhausted himself that he couldn't stand up on his legs at all, but sat sagged down with his weight on his breastbone, even after I let him out. So now if I must go out for any length of time the cage is covered with a dark cloth to make him go to sleep. He has to be coaxed into it with a dish of fresh seed, and you feel pretty mean when you shut the door.

He must sleep in the cage at night for his own

safety in a house where so much goes on, but he never goes there of his own accord. Each night when he has finally settled down on the top of a bookcase or lamp-shade I have to turn out the lights, pick him up, and set him on the perch in the cage, which ends in a little box, open at the front and bottom, fastened against the back wall. He doesn't really mind being picked up, but when he is wide awake he keeps just beyond your hovering hand. He will always step up on your finger, but will not allow your hand to close over him unless he is drowsy. He never flutters then, but turns his head and deliberately fastens his beak on your finger in a severe pinch. It's not fear. It's sheer malice. Face-saving.

When he has to be turned over and have his toe-nails clipped he cranes round to see what's going on, taking an occasional nip on your finger. It doesn't hurt to have his nails cut if you're careful, and he isn't afraid. But it infringes on his dignity, and he lets you know. Once when it went on a little too long and I was clumsy he let out his single alarm note—a low, sweet, minor *"Weeee!"* which I have heard only a few times, once when a foot came too near him on the floor, once when I tried to pull out a broken tail feather which was still firmly attached and it hurt.

He shows affection by little kiss-picks on your finger while he sits there—or the gentlest peck at your lips from a perch on your shoulder, when you can actually feel the warmth of his breath through his open beak.

The master said that wild birds shouldn't be allowed

to stuff seeds all day from a constant supply, because in the natural state they get hungry between meals and too much easy food and not enough exercise would mean a fatty heart. So I took to swiping Che-Wee's dish as soon as he left it after a good feed, and slipping it into the top middle drawer of my desk. We try not to deprive him of things by sheer virtue of our size, while he looks on helpless and aghast. He's allowed to finish his meal and then the dish sort of disappears. Pretty soon he misses it and hunts round briskly. That's funny, I had it here a little while ago. Ah, there's the orange-colored box the seeds come out of. He goes and sits on top of the box wistfully. Finally he must have help—flies down on my shoulder with his confidential "Teet-a-teet-teet?" I can't last. If he's hungry enough to say Please, he's hungry enough to get it.

He learned about the middle drawer of the desk, of course. He saw the seed dish go into it sometimes, he often saw it come out. My check-book and address-book are kept there too. If I open the drawer to get one of them he will fly down on the edge of it, daring me to close it on him, and with no trap-sense whatever will enter an opening no wider than his body to reach the seed dish within.

From the beginning he craved our company and missed us when we were gone. If we went outside to garden or drove into town to meet a train, and he was left alone in the house he rushed to meet us on our return, crest up, tail flirting, sat on shoulders, rained kiss-picks, registered joy. Being shut into one room because window screens were out or the family was going away was something he always tried to circumvent by getting through the door first, or lighting on top of it, convinced that it couldn't be closed if he was there. We have a family nightmare that he will get pinched in a closing door, and the situation is even worse in New York, where he has twice shot over somebody's head into the outer hall while the apartment door was open. The elevator has an open ironwork cage, and if he once got through it into the shaft we might never get him out alive. Both times so far he has lighted on the fire extinguishing apparatus and ridden back triumphantly on my finger. Both times I have nearly had heart failure.

So we taught him the rattle-box game. We put sunflower seeds in a plain, half-pint ice-cream carton—sunflower seeds are the chocolate creams in his life—and he learned very quickly that after the box was shaken the top came off and he was allowed to choose a seed. If you pick up the box and rattle it he will fly on to your hands with his "K-k-k-k-k!" and watch for the cover to be removed so that he can snatch his treat. This gives us some hope that if ever he does get out of bounds he will return to our hands, however frightening or confusing his surroundings may be, and he is rehearsed frequently with suitable rewards. Often in between times he is found sitting hopefully on the box, which has not made a sound.

5.

Dᴜʀɪɴɢ ᴛʜᴇ ᴡɪɴ-
ter months in the city he ate raw green peas, lettuce,
and cabbage for his greens, but we thought he needed a
playground. So we got a large baking-pan, filled it
with earth with a couple of nice rocks sticking out,
planted a small slab of turf in one corner, two tiny ever-

greens, and a few dry stalks of caraway like dead trees. We sank a little glass custard cup to its brim, to hold water for a pool, and Che-Wee had a garden.

As usual he joined in excitedly, picking at the earth and plants, scolding at the old spoon we used for a spade, asserting his property rights long before it was completed and turned over to him. He rooted up the bird seed we planted almost as fast as we could put it in, but some of it sprouted and was delicious. His sense of ownership on that bit of ground is perpetually aggressive. You are hardly allowed to water it without being warned off. One day I began to set out a new plant to replace a badly nibbled one at one end, and he charged me the length of the pan, chittering angrily, fell into the pool in his hurry, scrambled out and came on full tilt, jabbing at my fingers with his open beak.

The first time he saw snow he was fascinated and sat a long time in the window sill watching it come down in a whirling blizzard. He seemed to feel smugly secure and sheltered, with no need to take the same precautions he still does when rain beats against the window-pane.

By Christmas time he registered a scant ounce on my desk postal scales, and had taken to apartment life with the same happy philosophy with which he had accepted the Vermont farm house, and no more was said about the bird house at the Zoo. Nothing upset him. He was wakened once near midnight to be introduced to a British Air Marshal and his blue-clad staff, and he climbed composedly on to the Marshal's finger to sit surrounded by bigger and better wings than a purple finch ever saw before. He showed off his card trick to the President of the Zoological Society, who had never for one minute believed he could do it. He learned to drink milk turn-about with the master, balanced on the outer side of the tipped glass with his breast bumping the master's nose while he waited for it to be his turn to dip in.

He invented a game of his own. Always he would box with his open beak at a finger waved in front of him. But somehow we discovered that if we made pincers back at him with thumb and index finger he would allow his beak to be caught and with feet braced would tug himself free and come back for more. Apparently it was fun. If he hadn't enjoyed it he could have flown away. But over and over again he would jab and tug, pulling himself almost off his feet, jab and tug again.

As spring came on he began to sing—very softly, just above a whisper, with his beak still closed. But it was singing. Complicated, sweet, and sustained, but very shy, for there was no one to give him lessons. This seemed to me to settle the aspersions which had been cast on his possible sex. The book says purple finches do not always acquire their adult male plumage until the second or third year, so he had plenty of time. But he was singing. For accompaniment he liked a boiling teakettle or running water, and later a Hawaiian record on the victrola would usually set him off. The singing canaries on the radio he ignored with an almost visible boredom. Riff-raff. Professionals.

6.

IN LATE APRIL HE
migrated northward again, this time in a little wooden
travelling cage to which we had fitted a flannel jacket
to keep out draughts and make it dark. He was allowed
to get acquainted with the cage before the journey. We
left it on a table in my study, put seed and water in

its cups, let him go in and out. Once in a while I would close its door a few minutes while he was inside, and open it at once when he started to fuss. We felt it was important that he should never have a fright now, he had come so far without one.

This time the journey was made in a small car, on a warm spring day. We stopped at a roadside restaurant and took the cage inside with us. No fluttering. We stopped along the road for a picnic, took the jacket off the cage, and Che-Wee sat in the sun sheltered from a nippy wind and ate fresh grass and clover and hard-boiled egg yolk through the bars and drank from his water cup. Complete *sangfroid*, after hours of jolting along in the strange sound of a motor.

When he arrived inside the house he had first seen, he flew around busily, his crest high, his tail flirting, as though counting things up. His branches were still in the windows. He made sure of those. Ate seeds. Dropped off to sleep at twilight, but without retiring to his old alcove perch. I had shipped up a good-sized canary cage with a little box fitted over the upper perch, and at night he was put into that for safe-keeping, with a dark cloth laid over the whole. Even though it sits on the chest of drawers in the alcove, near his favorite branch and hook, he won't put himself to bed in it, but has to be collected and set there each night. I think he enjoys the game of biting my fingers as he goes. In the morning when the cloth is removed and the door is fastened open he rushes out with a God-blessmy-soul effect of delighted surprise at a new day, and flies up and down the house for his morning exercise.

As soon as it was warm enough I made the experiment of taking him outdoors in his cage. But the fact of being in a cage soon outweighed the sunshine and the interesting things I offered him to eat through the bars, and he was unhappy, so after a few attempts I gave it up. At the very end of the summer, when he was dumpy with moulting, I tried him again and he loved it—sat in the sun all spraddled out with his wings spread and every feather on end for a sun-bath, nibbled at what was given him and seemed not to feel captive at all.

The officious people who always know best are inclined to cross-examine us about our right to keep a bird in the house, and they raise the question of what would happen if we set him free (*sic*) and they imply that if he was really better off with us he would always come back of his own free will. I try to be patient with them, while reminding myself that like the fox who lost his tail and tried to persuade his friends to do without theirs, when you haven't got a bird you may subconsciously resent people who have. What would happen, quite simply, would be that within a few days Che-Wee would be very dead, of exposure or exhaustion or fright or even hunger. The first cold rain would be his certain end, if futile flight and bewilderment did not enter into it. We would be kinder to chloroform him than to leave him to make his own way in the bird world now. I haven't much doubt that he would want to come back home and try to—but strangeness and distance and loss of contact with all he is accustomed to might prevent this. If he is to live out his little span, his destiny runs with ours now, and he shows no knowledge of missing anything he is entitled to, not even the society of his peers.

In July, he encountered his first bird and as usual took his own surprising line. For some days we had been watching a nestful of five baby field sparrows in the mowing back of the house. The parent birds had built on the ground just under a charged wire running from the corner of the building which housed the electric light plant down past the vegetable garden, to keep the deer out. Work was being done on the building and people constantly passed that way along a path just inside the wire. We tried not to disturb the old birds, and sometimes one of them would remain on the nest, motionless, while we walked by. Sometimes it would leave the nest and hop along the ground several feet before taking off.

Making a service trip to feed oil to the engine one cold rainy day, I noticed that no bird flew up as I approached the nest, and the five babies, still very young, were exposed to the storm and looked as though they had been for some time. For the rest of the day we worried about them, and made several trips back to the nest without seeing a parent bird. At ten o'clock that night it was still raining, and we went out under an umbrella with a flashlight and collected the five drenched infants in a pan lined with flannel and brought them into the house. They still moved and opened their beaks with little hoarse cries, but you could almost wring water out of them. We fed them bread soaked in milk and covered them up where it was warm. We didn't want them, of course. But they would all have been dead by morning. We meant to try and raise them far enough for them to take care of themselves, and then out they went and no nonsense. At the back of my mind was the idea that we might keep just one, as company for Che-Wee.

The next morning they heard his wings when he flew out into the kitchen where their flannel-lined pan was, and they thought it was mamma and set up a howl for food, all five beaks opened wide. The sound seemed to stir no atavistic chord in Che-Wee's make-up. Usually so curious, he refused to take any interest in what went on around the pan, even when we fed them. It was as though he found the whole thing a trifle embarrassing and had decided not to n-o-t-i-c-e. He just went on about his own affairs and left the sparrows to theirs. A mob scene, he seemed to say. The lower orders. I can't be bothered. Let 'em eat cake.

Finally I set the strongest and noisiest of the little strangers on my finger and held it out to Che-Wee till it was within a few inches of him. He watched its approach nervously. When it had come near enough he flew away, decisively, into the next room and stayed there. Really, the thing had *feathers!* Surely he wasn't required to make friends with objects like that?

It would seem that Che-Wee has forgotten he is a bird. He thinks he's people. And he's about right, at that.

The sparrows didn't flourish noticeably, and one of them died, the littlest one. When the weather finally cleared, we put them out on the lawn in the sun in a wire cage. They yeeped around and didn't use their legs and didn't know enough to pick for themselves. They were younger than Che-Wee had been when we brought him in out of the storm, and their I.Q. was definitely lower.

With intense relief, we noticed what appeared to be one of the parent birds hovering around the cage. We tipped the wire netting over so that the babies were free on the grass, and retired into the middle distance and waited. The old bird led them off, one at a time, into the shadow under the lilac bush. We were more than willing that she should reassume the responsibility. The mystery of why the nest was left wide open to the elements for eight solid hours remains, along with the mystery of her wish to reclaim babies who had been handled and missing for several days.

So Che-Wee apparently doesn't miss the company of his own kind. If it had been a baby purple finch I offered to his notice he might have relented, who knows? But as for sparrows, he was ag'in 'em.

One dim little instinct does still prevail and I confess

it makes my heart ache. He collects things to build a nest with. Bits of stick and straw are carried round, rather aimlessly, and then lost track of, thread or string is busily gathered up, loop on expert loop across his bill, till the last dragging end is clear of his feet—and then there is a puzzled sort of pause—let's see, now, what was I going to do with this?—oh, well—and the treasure is abandoned and forgotten.

7.

H<small>IS</small> REACTIONS TO family life are often similar to what might be expected of a dog, but hardly of a bird—his sense, amounting to foreboding, of our impending departures from the house, his joy at our returns, his apparent responsibility for some one who lies down to rest. The protective attitude was brought still more to the fore when during the summer I slipped on the stairs and damaged an ankle, which had to be put in a cast.

Che-Wee was sitting on the back of the sofa where I lay when the doctor arrived with the materials for the cast—a cardboard carton with a big roll of cotton sticking out the top, and the heavy plaster bandages and the tools. The doctor set the things out on a bridge table near by, hot water was brought in a basin, and he set about the tedious task of padding the leg with cotton and winding the soaked bandage. Che-Wee watched anxiously and came down on my shoulder for a better view. Then he flew on to the table and peered from there, until I thought he might even light on the doctor's hands. But the man was after all a stranger, and Che-Wee doesn't fraternize easily.

Somewhere midway of the job he decided that everything was under control and went up to the edge of the carton to investigate that, and took a pull at the cotton. A minute later we looked round to find him waiting for his laugh with a square white Santa Claus beard of cotton sticking out all round his bill. We roared with amusement, and he dropped his act and the cotton and returned to the sofa, satisfied.

He does seem sometimes deliberately to clown. He handles a tooth pick like a drum major, running it back and forth in his beak with great speed and skill, or hopping along the floor with it cocked end-on like a Rooseveltian cigarette-holder. During the long days when I

had to sit with my foot up on a hassock, a foot swathed
in a heavy cast with a knitted bedsock over that and a
rug over the whole, he used the football-shaped object
as a favorite perch and often did his feathers sitting
there while I read or wrote on a lap-board. The best
laugh I had was once when I lost track of him, guessed
that he was on the floor, and ordered him out into view,
because he is too near the color of the rug and too fear-
less for safety. "Che-Wee, up off the floor!" I said
forcefully, and he arrived briskly from somewhere below and round the corner on to my extended foot. He
had a long grass-blade held crosswise in his beak, like
the rose in Carmen's teeth, and he held the pose smugly
while I shouted with joy. Unlike a dog, he seems to
enjoy being laughed at, and regards himself as a success
when it happens.

He never misses a chance to perch conspicuously on
the top of a rum or sherry bottle, looking a little self-
conscious and clever. He will pick somebody sitting
with his knees crossed and work industriously at the
task of untieing the shoelace, with surprisingly stout
tugs which set him right back on his heels. He makes a
terrific fuss about keeping his footing on something
slippery or unsteady, as though he had no wings to save
himself from a fall. And the daily business of dressing
his feathers produces contortions and undignified posi-
tions of infinite variety and foolishness. One evening he
played for some time with a dead leaf, tossing it over his
head by the stem and flourishing it round like a signal

flag, while a large audience applauded and giggled. The next day the dead leaf was still there where he had left it, and after a few tentative passes at it—this was good for a laugh last night—he went into the act again, like the little ham he is, though nobody but me was present to be entertained.

We have been very careful of his health and have had few scares. His cage is covered against draughts at night, and his food is kept as simple as possible with no grease and almost no sweet, though he has recently discovered what lives in the sugar bowl and goes for it if he gets a chance.

Once he seemed to have a chill, and sat all day on his branch with his eyes half closed, swaying a little on spraddled legs. I had foreseen from the beginning that a time must come when some such thing must begin, but now that it appeared to be here I could only think Not Yet, Not *Already!* I spent most of that day coaxing him to take a little orange juice, a little milk, from a spoon—seeds were beyond him. When I put him in the cage that night he seemed nothing but feathers in my hand—no warmth, no weight to him at all.

The next morning I set my teeth and took the cloth off the cage, and Che-Wee was still there on the perch, able to come down to the door under his own power. He ate a few greens that day, and drank more milk and didn't wobble so much. The following day he was as good as new. He might have caught a spider or a fly around the windows that didn't agree with him, or he might have taken cold. Whatever it was, he dealt with it, and became even a little more precious as his high spirits returned.

Some time after that he began to itch most dretfully, and scratched behind his ears with first one foot and then the other till I thought he would be raw. He drooped and moped and his legs seemed tired and his vitality low, and when he came on your finger there was no grip to his toes. We did what you do for mites —cleaned and sterilized his cage, and sunned it, put cotton on the ends of the perches, used a magnifying glass for traces—nothing. We did what you do for lice, which was to pump insect powder into his feathers with a medicine dropper—he hated it. And he went right on scratching and moping. And then I thought, Moulting?

The master was away again so I wrote to the Zoo in New York and received a kindly treatise back from the Curator of Birds on what the trouble might be and what to do. He thought it was probably moult, which always made birds limp and wretched.

Che-Wee was inclined to go off by himself now, and he spent a great deal of time in holes and corners combing out his feathers. Soon, below where he had sat, there would be a little pile of discarded fluff and quills, and we noticed that when he pulled a feather out in his beak, however small and downy, he always laid it down with the utmost care on the perch beside him, as though he might want it again, even though it drifted away at once.

He needed a new coat, as he had broken off most of his tail feathers bumping into window sills and so on, and he had trouble steering himself when he flew. Otherwise he had kept neat and smooth and never looked shabby. His crest went first, so that he was flat-headed and bald-looking, with little whitish bristles—and there was no laughter, no gaiety about him any more. Then his last few tail quills went, so that he was completely bobbed and very clumsy in his flight, but almost immediately the tips of new quills began to show and grew very fast. His wing coverts replaced themselves almost over night, with bright tan edges and a more pronounced pattern. Then for a long time he looked as though he had a string tied round his neck where his mane was missing. And then his face was all pin-feathers, which made his eyes bug out.

All this time he seemed to know that he was not looking his best, and sat disconsolately on the edges of waste-paper baskets and the lower rungs of chairs and worked piteously at his feathers. No singing now, of course. And at the same time he was lonesome, and had never been so docile and so friendly and inclined to sit close by when anybody read or wrote. He had bad days, worse than others, when his legs wouldn't hold him up and he sat about on his breastbone. He labored endlessly at himself, picking at his wings and shoulders and tail and back, standing very tall in order to reach the distant spot between his legs. His contortions were pretty funny, and yet he was so earnest and so worried you couldn't laugh.

Quite suddenly, when his new tail had reached its approximate length, and his new wing quills were all in line, and his breast was plump and soft with wonderful new plumage, Che-Wee was himself again—brisk, independent, and gay. He had got his new suit and was proud of it. True, it wasn't the port-colored satin his father wore in the cherry hedge a year ago, and unkind people still made disparaging remarks which cast doubts on his masculinity. His answer to that is mainly his song—stronger now, and more complicated, but still shy and sweet, with quavery trills and deep contralto notes. A certain unkind ornithologist has suggested that Che-Wee had better read up on his own biographies, where it says: "Sometimes in late May or early June he may be heard to burst forth as if with unrestrained emotion so suddenly as to startle one by the gushing of his overpowering melody. I have thought sometimes that it was the most impassioned bird song that we have in our groves and woodlands." But Che-Wee is still very young and inexperienced, and there has been no one to teach him the family melody, he has only what he can remember from the time when he was an egg.

The books say females do not sing, and that when a brown purple finch has been observed to do so it is a mistake to assume that it is a female—it is a he-finch who is still wearing his immature plumage. And in captivity the color is supposed never to be so bright, and sometimes fades to the look of a drab canary. There is nothing drab about Che-Wee's new suit, and it has a distinctly rosy cast across the breast and on the rump. The master is merely trying to get a rise out of us when he says that one resembles a rather dirty English sparrow.

8.

KIPLING, WHO AL-
ways knew what he was talking about, has written more
than once about the sure retribution which follows if
you let your heart be caught by creatures whose little
life span is bound to end too soon and leave you deso-
late and inconsolable. I, in my time, have been some-

what impatient with some too-articulate woman's grief over the loss of a pet dog or cat, which seemed to me excessive and dramatized for any sensible grown-up. From the day Che-Wee first entered the house we were firm in our determination that he was not going to spell tragedy, that we would remember that he was a bird and that we couldn't keep him long, and that we would neither dread his departure from our lives nor mourn unduly when that occurred. As time goes on there is less and less of this stout talk.

As a child I read *Black Beauty* and *Dicky Downy* and some horrible tale about a little dog who had to have its ears and tail docked to be in the fashion. I read them unwillingly, but with a dreadful fascination, knowing that they must end in the most lachrymose fatalities. Let me say at once that you need not be afraid to come to the end of this story. Che-Wee is still with us and still full of beans.

But we must admit that he becomes more enchanting each day, now that the moult has passed and he is himself again. His own delight in mere life has a touching quality that cannot be denied. He stands so tall on his little stick legs, with his knickerbockers showing. His wings are held so briskly with their tips just crossed above the base of his forked tail. His fragile, foolish feet have such variety of comic expression—pigeon-toed with effort as he digs for an apple seed, placed with affected grace on the edge of a dish like a little finger crooked above a teacup, heels hooked tight at other times for leverage, or the curled, helpless look of the one which is hoisted pensively into his feathers in his moments of reposeful listening to conversation or music; the making of his elaborate toilet, which takes place several times a day, when each feather is combed out and dressed, and wings are held at impossible angles so their inner sides can be got at with the beak, and the region between the legs and above the tail must be stretched for and groomed.

He has formed little habits and routines of his own, like always coming into my room in the morning to sit on the top of the hand-mirror and preen himself while I am putting on a face and doing up my hair for the day—face powder and mascara apparently taste delicious, but they can't be described as natural food for a bird, and so he has to be fended off from pilfering, which makes for continual argument and delay. He is irresistibly confident of his welcome, even when he is being a nuisance, so innocent of inferiorities and rancor, and he never holds a grudge if he is accidentally startled or brushed off by somebody who hasn't seen him in time. He didn't hold it against me when he flew into the invisible hairnet I had spread between my hands, and it took ten minutes to cut him out of it, entangled as it was in his claws and around his beak and tail. When I set him free again, on the back of a chair his crest immediately rose—well, *that's* over!— and he accepted a sunflower seed as consolation with no sulks at all. And daily his song increases, brave and sweet and solitary, his little gift to the household which shelters him.

Canaries live into their teens, and he is cousin to canaries, though he would doubtless deny the connection. With luck, we can expect to have this affectionate, humorous, and unconsciously pathetic little presence about the house for a decade. But already I have learned what it is to uncover his cage in the morning with an anxiety which all my good sense and fine resolves tell me is disproportionate. Mature philosophy isn't any good, as Kipling well knew with his dogs. Che-Wee has won. He has us all by the heart. His dignity, his insouciance, his busy flights past our heads, his inquiring arrivals into a conversation, late, with a what-are-we-taking-about-now effect—above all his touching confidence in our wisdom and good intentions towards himself—there is no possible answer to him but a foolish devotion on our part which is way beyond his size.

He is so small to be so gallant—so frail to be so dauntless. The nearest he comes to fear is a sort of wary curiosity which makes him stand very tall with his legs and neck stretched to their laughable limit, while he tries to see what makes the funny noise or whatever it is that seems to him unusual. On the rare occasions when he has to be pursued because he has stolen something he must not eat or because he must be caught and put in the cage, he turns the chase into a hilarious game, crest erect, tail flirting, peering down from inaccessible places at the exasperated person below. The few small alarms he has ever known have turned at once into triumphs—hunh! never touched *me!* Clever me. Happy me. Safe and cherished, invulnerable, unmolestable me. I got folks, I have, nothing can happen to *me*. Pigeons, sparrows, down there in the street—they got to be careful and watch out for themselves. Outdoors birds in the country—they make nests on the ground, they fall out of trees, they got to worry about mowing machines and owls and cats. I got no worries. I got folks. Howsabout us cutting up an apple?